SURVIVAL.

Ice Storm!

Frieda Wishinsky

Illustrated by
Don Kilby

Scholastic Canada Ltd.

Toronto New York London Auckland Sydney
Mexico City New Delhi Hong Kong Buenos Aires

Scholastic Canada Ltd.
604 King Street West, Toronto, Ontario M5V 1E1, Canada

Scholastic Inc.
557 Broadway, New York, NY 10012, USA

Scholastic Australia Pty Limited
PO Box 579, Gosford, NSW 2250, Australia

Scholastic New Zealand Limited
Private Bag 94407, Botany, Manukau 2163, New Zealand

Scholastic Children's Books
Euston House, 24 Eversholt Street, London NW1 1DB, UK

www.scholastic.ca

Library and Archives Canada Cataloguing in Publication
Wishinsky, Frieda, author
  Ice storm! : the great storm of 1998 / Frieda Wishinsky ; illustrated
by Don Kilby.
(Survival)
Issued in print and electronic formats.
ISBN 978-1-4431-4647-0 (paperback).--ISBN 978-1-4431-4648-7 (html)
  I. Kilby, Don, illustrator II. Title. III. Series: Wishinsky, Frieda.
Survival.
PS8595.I834I24 2016   jC813'.54   C2016-902807-0

Photo credits: cover: Boris Spremo/Canadian Press Images; 102: Erin
Murray/Public Safety Canada.

6 5 4 3 2 1 Printed in Canada 121 17 18 19 20 21

MIX
Paper from
responsible sources
FSC® C004071

For my friend Karen Krossing

CHAPTER ONE

January 7, 1998

Ethan glanced up and down the street.

He had to find help. But how could he leave Sylvie and Mrs. Greenbaum in the freezing cold?

A wave of dizziness rolled over Ethan. He stopped to take a breath. Drops of freezing rain flew into his face and eyes, making it hard to breathe. Sharp ice pellets stung like needles against his cheek.

The houses on their block were draped in coats of thick white ice. They looked like they were splattered in layers of icing. Icicles the size of swords hung down from the roofs, the entrances, the balconies and the window ledges.

Trees were bent over. Some had snapped in half. Huge limbs had crashed down on frozen, buried cars, garbage cans and mailboxes. The cars that weren't damaged lay abandoned and useless under the heavy ice.

The streets looked like a world of endless winter — a world where all the people had disappeared.

Ethan shivered. The cold pierced through his jacket and pants.

The ground was as slick as glass. Every step made him feel like he'd slide across the ice on his back.

The wind whistled in his ears and the freezing rain kept coming down as he crossed the street to Rafi's building.

He was about to press the apartment buzzer when it hit him: the bell wouldn't work without power.

He banged hard on the door, hoping that someone inside would somehow hear him. But no one came to the door.

He would have to look for help on the main street instead!

He was about to cross the street when a chunk of sharp ice crashed down in front of him.

Ethan stumbled and fell to the ground.

CHAPTER TWO

January 6, 1998

"Don't worry, Dad," said Ethan. "We'll be fine . . . Yes. I promise. See you tonight." Ethan handed the phone to his stepmother.

"It's just a bad storm, Jon," said Sylvie. "I've been through lots of storms . . . Don't worry . . . that's weeks away . . . Yes . . . I love you, too."

Sylvie hung up the phone and poured herself another cup of tea.

"I have to hurry," Ethan said, pulling on his boots. "My teacher gets mad if we're late."

"It's miserable and cold out there. Don't forget your tuque and gloves. Here, take an extra sweater," said Sylvie, brushing her blond bangs out of her eyes.

"I don't need an extra sweater," said Ethan. "I'm fine."

"But it's colder and icier than usual today. You have to be careful walking to school. I'm staying home today to get this ad done before my deadline, but I wouldn't want to go out unless I absolutely had to." Sylvie was a graphic designer and often worked from home.

"Well I *have* to go to school today, so that's that." Ethan hated being told what to wear and what to do all the time. He hated that Sylvie was always telling him to be careful. He wasn't a little kid! He was twelve. "Don't worry about me. I know how to get around on ice."

Ethan grabbed his dark grey backpack and headed out the door of their second-floor apartment. This was the second time his dad had travelled for work since he and Sylvie were married a year ago, and it felt strange staying alone in the apartment with his stepmother. He still felt like she was a visitor sleeping over, not a part of his family. He tried to be polite, but he always had to hold back the words he wanted to say. His dad would be upset if Ethan told Sylvie what he really thought — that she wasn't his mom and he didn't need her advice.

Why did Dad have to get married again? thought Ethan. They had been fine on their own. They had done everything together, until his dad met Sylvie.

In a few weeks there would be a new baby in their small two-bedroom apartment — Ethan's half-sister. Now there'd be two strangers living with him, and one would be crying all the time. His best friend Rafi said his little brother Jose used to cry so much that Rafi put cotton balls in his ears to block out the sound.

Ethan sighed as he hurried down the stairs. If only his mom were here. He missed her every day, but most of all when his dad was away.

She had died a year after they moved to Montreal from Toronto. And even though three years had passed, Ethan still imagined his mom waiting for him outside the school at the end of the day. He could almost see her greeting him with her wide smile and twinkling eyes. Everyone said that Ethan had the same deep green eyes as his mom and that he had her bumpy nose, too.

His parents had planned to start looking for a house to buy in Montreal, but then his mom got sick and everything changed. Now Sylvie and his dad were going to look for a house in the spring. Until then they were all stuck in this small apartment in an older house.

As Ethan reached the first floor, the door to Apartment 1 opened and a white-haired woman bundled in a furry black coat and hat stepped out. She held a grey cane in one hand and locked her door with the other.

"Hi, Mrs. Greenbaum," Ethan said, smiling.

Mrs. Greenbaum turned and smiled back. "Hello, Ethan! Are you off to school? I'm just going to the corner store for milk and bread."

"It's nasty outside. We have milk and bread in our apartment if you want. Or I could pick some up for you after school. You don't have to go out."

Mrs. Greenbaum patted Ethan on the back. "It's kind of you to be concerned about me, but it's good for me to get out — even in bad weather. The weatherman says it will only get worse later. My cane has a sharp point to dig into the ice." Mrs. Greenbaum held up the bottom of her cane. "I bought it for weather just like this."

"That's a cool cane."

"It's a wonderful idea but I wish I didn't need a cane. What can you do? Since my knee surgery, it's harder to walk. I used to be such a good ice-skater. Remember when I took you ice-skating when you first moved to Montreal? You took to the ice like a duck to water." Ethan had known Mrs.

Greenbaum since he'd moved into the house. When his mother was sick, she'd helped look after him.

Ethan laughed. "I fell a hundred times that first day, but you kept telling me to get up and try again."

"And you did. Now you skate like a champion. I'm afraid that my skating days are over." Mrs. Greenbaum shrugged her shoulders and sighed. Then she straightened up and smiled again. "But not my walking days! I can manage half a block with this cane, even on ice!"

Ethan grinned. "I know. Nothing stops you, Mrs. Greenbaum, but please be careful."

"Believe me, I don't want to break my other leg. One broken leg is enough for a lifetime."

"I'll see you later. I have to run or I'll be late for school"

"Don't run, Ethan. Not today!"

Ethan laughed. "You sound like Sylvie. But I'll be okay. Don't worry!"

"I know, but what can I say. You're like my grand-son, and grandmothers worry. Have a good day."

Ethan waved and reached for the front door.

As soon as he pushed the door open, a blast of cold rain blew into Ethan's face. He shivered and hunched over as freezing drops hit his jacket and hood.

The sky was a dull grey. The streets and sidewalks were coated in ice. Everything glistened — utility poles, trees, house and building roofs, mailboxes and garbage cans. The shimmering whiteness of everything was beautiful. If only it weren't so cold and slippery.

Suddenly a car skidded so close that Ethan had to jump over a frozen tree limb to get out of the way. His heart pounded as he slid on a chunk of ice and almost fell. He straightened out when he heard a cry. He spun around.

Oh no!

It was Mrs. Greenbaum! She'd fallen on the icy ground.

CHAPTER THREE

Ethan rushed down the street. Mrs. Greenbaum had slipped near an ice-covered mailbox and was now on the ground, leaning against it.

"Are you okay?" he asked.

"I need . . . a minute to catch my breath. My legs flew out from under me. Could you hand me my cane? It's over there." She pointed to the spot on the road where her cane had landed.

Ethan handed Mrs. Greenbaum her cane.

"Can you stand up?" he asked.

"Yes. I think so." She dug her cane into the ice. Then she tried to push herself up.

"Here. Let me help you." Ethan extended his hand.

"Thank you." Mrs. Greenbaum grabbed Ethan's

hand. Ethan used his other hand to support her upper arm as she leaned in and stood up. "It's good I wore thick gloves and a big fur coat. They saved me from a worse fall," she said.

"I can help you walk back to the building."

"It's only a few more steps to the store. I can manage. I will be more careful. Go on. I don't want you to be late for school."

Mrs. Greenbaum leaned on her cane and took a step forward. She wobbled and clutched her cane tighter. Ethan watched as she took a second step and a third. She stopped and steadied herself against a row of newspaper boxes, but she didn't turn back. She moved forward slowly, one step at a time.

"Go to school, Ethan. I'm fine," she called.

"I'll wait until you make it to the store," Ethan called back.

A few more steps and Mrs. Greenbaum reached the store. She looked back at Ethan. "See! I made it. Now go!" She waved him on, and he turned down the street toward his school.

He checked his watch. He *was* going to be late, but his teacher, Ms. Lee, couldn't be mad on a day like today!

As soon as he reached his class, he saw that Ms. Lee was late, too. The vice-principal was sitting at her desk. Only half of the kids had made it to school, but Ethan's best friend Rafi was there. Rafi lived across the street from Ethan and they always walked home together after school. Rafi and Ethan had been friends ever since Ethan had moved to Montreal.

Ms. Lee finally arrived an hour after school had started. They were all reading when she walked into class. The vice-principal had given them silent reading time, and Ms. Lee gave them twenty minutes more to read. Then they began working on a winter art collage.

Ethan turned to Rafi and said, "This is fun. I

wish we could do art like this every day." Ethan stuck bits of white tissue paper on the giant tree he'd drawn.

"I like your collage," said Rafi. "Your tree looks like a creature with spiky white tentacles."

Ethan laughed. "You're right."

The rest of the day zoomed by with math and science. Then the home bell rang.

The boys grabbed their backpacks.

"Listen to that," said Rafi, as they left the school building. Ice crashed down from nearby trees like shatterd glass. "I've never heard anything like it before."

"Check out those crazy icicles," Ethan said, pointing to the roof of a nearby house. "And look at that tree. It looks like the creature from my collage with those icy broken branches dangling off it."

Rafi bent his arms over like the tree, contorted his face into a grimace and stomped across the ice. "This is how your creature walks."

"Or slides!" said Ethan, mimicking the expression on Rafi's face and sliding across the ice.

Rafi sailed across the ice after him. "Sliding on ice is the only thing I like about winter. I don't think I'll ever get used to how cold it is."

"You were lucky to live in a warm place like Mexico. We visited the Yucatan over Christmas vacation before my mom got sick. We even climbed some narrow old stairs up to the top of one of the Mayan ruins. You could see everything from up there."

"Hey, I went to the Yucatan with my mom and dad when I was a little kid, too. My mom took two weeks off from her job at the hospital. That was way before my parents split up." Rafi sighed. Then he slid across another patch of ice. "*Wueeeee*," he called.

Ethan slid across the ice after him, but as he did, he collided with a man hurrying down the icy street, clutching a briefcase. The briefcase fell as the man tried to regain his footing.

"Sorry," said Ethan.

"Watch where you're going or someone will get hurt," the man grumbled, picking up his briefcase. He rushed off down the street.

"He didn't sound happy," said Rafi.

"No one's happy today."

"The only person who likes this weather is Jose. He wants me to build an iceman with him. He was asking to build one today, but Mom made him stay home from kindergarten 'cause he has a bad cold."

"I bet we'll all stay home tomorrow if this keeps up."

The boys reached the corner of their block.

"See you," said Ethan, waving to his friend.

Ethan stepped over a mound of ice and crossed the street. There were fewer cars on the road than there had been that morning and fewer people were walking on the slick streets.

Ice pellets swirled around him and flew into his face. He pulled his hood tighter around his head. It was so cold, and it didn't seem to be letting up.

CHAPTER FOUR

Warm air enveloped Ethan like a blanket as he stepped inside the narrow hall of the triplex. He unzipped his jacket and untied his dripping hood. As he turned toward the stairs, Mrs. Greenbaum opened her door. She had her favourite cane, which she often used to get around indoors, in one hand. This one was decorated with butterfly stickers.

Mrs. Greenbaum looked on the hall table where the mail was usually placed. "I wonder if the mailman can get through today. How is it outside now?" she asked.

"Worse than this morning. How was your walk back from the store?"

"I was glad to have my winter cane. It helped

me make it back in one piece. I hope you weren't late for school."

"I was late, but so was my teacher and a bunch of other kids. Did they have ice storms like this when you were growing up in Russia?"

"I don't remember an ice storm like this one. All I remember are snowy days when the trees were draped in white like a bride. My friends and I loved building snowmen on days like that. Coming to

Montreal and living with winter here was not such a shock for me. But today the weather is bad, especially for someone with unsteady legs. Do you think you will have school tomorrow?"

"They told us to listen to the radio in the morning."

"If you're home, come for tea. I made sugar cookies today — your favourite."

"I love your cookies," said Ethan. "And your stories remind me of my grandmother's, except that she grew up on a farm in Ontario. She tells good stories, too. When she was a kid she had to feed the chickens in winter. She hated going into the cold coop, and the chickens weren't crazy about it either."

"I didn't grow up with chickens, but I once had to pluck a chicken my mother brought home from the market. For a few years after that, whenever my mother cooked chicken I felt sick to my stomach," said Mrs. Greenbaum. "I hope Sylvie's not going outside in this weather."

"No, she stayed home today. See you, Mrs. Greenbaum."

As soon as Ethan opened the door to his apartment, Sylvie called out, "Hello. I'm glad you're back."

Sylvie was sitting on a chair in the dining room, with her feet propped up on another chair. Her drawing board was perched on the glass-and-metal dining-room table. Papers, markers, pens and pencils were spread out across the table and the black leather couch.

She looked up from her drawing board. "It looks like the storm is getting worse out there. How was school?"

"Okay."

"I hope you accomplished more than I did today. It was hard to concentrate with the ice and wind rattling the windows. How was the walk home?"

"Cold and icy." Ethan dropped his backpack on the kitchen floor and helped himself to a glass of milk.

"I hope you were careful. You don't want to fall on the ice and break an arm or a leg."

"I know how to walk," said Ethan. He tried to keep his voice steady, but he hated how Sylvie always reminded him to be careful. He didn't need to be told the same thing over and over. When he'd complained to his dad that she kept treating him like a little kid and giving him advice, his dad just said it was because she cared.

But his mom had cared about him and she had never nagged him like that, even when he was little.

Ethan walked over to the large picture window in their living room. Half the glass was laced with ice. It looked like a giant spiderweb.

Ethan peered out. The roofs and sides of the houses and the two five-storey apartment buildings on their block were crusted with thick ice. Front yards looked like small frozen lakes surrounded by jagged white bushes. Some trees bent over from the weight of the ice, and a few utility poles leaned toward the ground. Power and cable lines dipped so low they looked like they were glued down to the frozen surface.

All along the street, parked cars were like giant lumps of ice. You'd need a sledgehammer to dig them out.

A smashing sound made Ethan jump. A chunk of ice from a nearby roof had crashed to the ground. Luckily no one had been standing there. Getting hit by a slab of falling ice would be brutal.

"Every time a slab of ice fell, I thought of the people in the streets below," said Sylvie. "It made me worry about you walking home from school."

"I told you, Sylvie, you don't have to worry about me," said Ethan. His voice was rising. He knew he was almost shouting, but he couldn't help it. "I'm almost thirteen."

"Well, not for ten months. But you're right. I do worry a lot, especially now with this baby on the way."

"You don't have to worry about *me*. Anyway, have you listened to the radio? What's the latest weather report?"

"The reporter said it would probably get worse tomorrow."

The phone rang.

"I'll get it," said Sylvie.

Ethan knew it was his dad from the way Sylvie's eyes lit up. But then her face fell.

"Oh no, Jon," said Sylvie. "You think your flight tonight will be cancelled? What about the train? . . . I see . . . Yes, we'll be okay . . . Hold on . . . Ethan, your dad wants to speak to you."

Sylvie handed Ethan the phone and walked into the kitchen. "Yes, Dad. I promise . . . I'll help Sylvie, but we're both fine. It's just a storm . . . Don't worry. See you soon."

Ethan hung up the phone and sighed. He wished his dad were coming home. He wished he didn't have to stay home alone with Sylvie again.

CHAPTER FIVE

Ethan sank down onto the couch beside a pile of Sylvie's art supplies. He picked up a sports magazine from the antique pine trunk they used as a coffee table and began reading. As he turned a page, the lights in the apartment flickered. They went on and off a few times before going out completely. Ethan tried to keep reading, but the sun was about to set and the light was dim.

Ethan put down his magazine and walked over to the window.

It wasn't just their house that had lost power; it looked like all the nearby houses and buildings had lost power, too.

Sylvie sighed. "I hope this doesn't last very long. I have a tight deadline and I can't work without light." She pulled a flashlight and a wind-up, battery-powered radio from the top shelf of the kitchen closet.

Ethan collected four thick candles from the utility closet in the hall. Sylvie liked candles and they had a good supply of them in all different sizes and colours. "It's going to get cold in here if the power doesn't come back on soon," he said.

"You're right." Sylvie lifted three blankets out of the trunk and piled them on a living-room chair.

"Do you think the whole city lost power?" asked Ethan.

"I hope not. Maybe it's just our neighbourhood. Let's listen to the radio."

Ethan wound up the radio his dad had bought for power outages. He fiddled with the dials until he found a local station.

"Freezing rain and ice are pummelling the city," said the announcer. *"There are power outages across Montreal, with some areas more affected than*

others. *Flights, trains and buses into and out of the city are cancelled.*

"Police advise residents to stay home or seek shelter with friends or relatives who have power. Driving conditions are dangerous and some roads are impassable. All bridges are closed due to heavy winds and icy conditions."

The announcer mentioned different areas in the city that had lost power, including their own.

"Hydro-Québec is working to restore power, but as the freezing rain continues that becomes increasingly difficult," he said. *"More areas of Montreal may lose power tonight. It's unclear when power will be restored."*

"Oh no," said Sylvie.

"Should we put some food outside on the balcony so it doesn't spoil?" suggested Ethan.

"Good thinking. I have a cooler in the closet."

Ethan got the cooler out from the back of the utility closet. He and Sylvie filled it with food from the fridge. Then Ethan dragged it over to the door leading to the balcony.

"The door is frozen," he said, trying to yank it open. Ethan jiggled the door until it creaked open. A blast of cold air hit his face as he looked out. The balcony had just enough room for a small table, four chairs and a few plant pots. Everything was covered with ice. The row of tall maple trees the balcony overlooked had turned bright yellow in the fall and were now glistening white. Branches that had snapped off from the weight of the ice littered the parking area behind the house.

The balcony floor was a sheet of ice. Ethan shoved the cooler to the side closest to the door. Then he shut the door.

"Thanks, Ethan," said Sylvie, as she flipped the switch on her flashlight. "What's wrong with this thing?" She jiggled it. "I hope it's not the batteries. I don't think we have any more."

"I have another flashlight in my room," said Ethan.

"You do?"

"I use it to read in bed at night."

Sylvie laughed. "I used to do that too when I was your age. My mother was strict about lights out when I was a kid."

"It's going to be hard to do my homework with no electricity."

"I'm sure your teacher doesn't expect anyone to do homework tonight."

"They used to read and write by candlelight in the old days," said Ethan. "I learned about that in history."

"I don't know how they did it. Reading by candle-light gives me a headache."

Ethan nodded. Sylvie was right about that. He had to squint to see the words in his magazine when he tried reading by candlelight. It hurt his eyes.

It was almost dark.

"Can you light the candles while I see what we have to eat?" asked Sylvie.

"Sure," Ethan said, fishing a box of matches out of a drawer.

"Make sure there's a dish under the candles. We don't want them to tip by accident. A fire is the last thing we need."

"I *know*," said Ethan. He knew he sounded annoyed, but why did Sylvie always have to lecture him?

Sylvie pulled out a box of crackers, peanut butter and jam. She sliced an apple and a pear.

Then they sat at the kitchen table. The candles flickered and cast strange shadows on the walls as they nibbled on the snacks and listened to more radio reports.

"The weather department predicts a couple of very tough days for Montreal, other parts of Quebec, Ontario and parts of the US," said the announcer. *"With bridges closed, the island of Montreal may be cut off from the world for days."*

CHAPTER SIX

"Days? Your dad might not be able to get home any time soon," said Sylvie. She closed her eyes and bit her lip. Ethan could tell that she was trying not to cry. "Sorry that I'm being so emotional. It's just with the baby and all . . ."

"We'll be fine," said Ethan, but a knot was forming in his stomach at the thought of days without power and with Sylvie. "They're not always right about the weather," he said.

"Don't forget to check on your elderly neighbours," the announcer continued.

"Mrs. Greenbaum!" said Ethan. "I want to go down and see if she's okay."

"Of course. But don't be long," said Sylvie. "Please."

"I'm only going downstairs. I'll be back in a few minutes. I promise."

"I know. It's just . . . it's strange here without your dad, without power and with this crazy storm."

Ethan grabbed his flashlight and opened the door of the apartment. The hall was dark. The wind howled outside. The window on the landing rattled in the freezing rain.

A loud cracking sound made Ethan jump. He pictured more ice falling off roofs onto cars and breaking tree branches and limbs. He imagined phone and electrical wires snapping off and hitting the frozen ground.

Ethan flashed the light ahead of him and slowly made his way down the stairs. It was dark and strangely quiet. Their neighbour Joe, who lived in the basement apartment, was away for the month. So it was only the three of them in the building.

Ethan's footsteps on the steep wooden stairs echoed as he made his way down to the first floor.

He knocked on Mrs. Greenbaum's door.

No answer.

He knocked again, louder. He heard tapping and then Mrs. Greenbaum said, "Who is it, please?" She sounded shaky and uncertain.

"It's Ethan."

The door opened. Mrs. Greenbaum stood there in a long red bathrobe, which covered her black pants and black turtleneck sweater. She leaned on her butterfly cane, a flashlight tucked under her arm. Mimi, her fluffy black-and-white cat, purred beside her.

"Ethan, I am so glad to see you. Come in. Please."

Ethan patted Mimi and followed Mrs. Greenbaum into the dark apartment. Down the hall he could see candles glowing in the living room. A short, fat blue candle filled a shallow glass dish on her mahogany dining-room table. Beside it stood her white

Sabbath candles in their silver candlesticks. Mrs. Greenbaum usually lit her Sabbath candles only on Friday nights. The candles looked beautiful in the ornate candlesticks, but they didn't cast much light and they wouldn't last very long either.

"Do you have enough food?" asked Ethan.

"I have enough for now. Thank you. It is strange to be alone in the dark, and I'm afraid my flashlight isn't very strong."

"You don't have to be alone. Come upstairs and stay with us."

"I . . . I don't want to bother you and Sylvie. She has enough to worry about with the baby on the way. And I know she is allergic to cats."

"Sylvie will be glad you came. I know she will. And Mimi will be fine for one night. Please, Mrs. Greenbaum, you have to come. I'll sleep on the couch and you can have my bed."

"You're a good boy, Ethan, and I appreciate this but . . ."

"Please, Mrs. Greenbaum. I'll worry about you and that won't be good either."

Mrs. Greenbaum patted Ethan on the shoulder. "You make a good argument. Okay, I'll come. First let me make sure Mimi has enough to eat and drink."

As Ethan waited for Mrs. Greenbaum to get ready, he sat on her blue-and-white flowered couch and watched the Sabbath candles cast a dim light on the dining room. How many candles did she even have left? He was glad she'd agreed to stay with them.

Only a few weeks earlier, he'd sipped lemon-and-honey tea and nibbled on homemade sugar cookies at that table. It was a sunny Sunday afternoon, and Mrs. Greenbaum had told him a story about when she first came to Canada and got lost in Montreal in the winter.

Who would have imagined that a few weeks later they'd be in the dark in the middle of a brutal ice storm?

CHAPTER SEVEN

Mrs. Greenbaum filled Mimi's bowls with water and food. Mimi rubbed against her leg and purred. She looked up and meowed as if she understood Mrs. Greenbaum was leaving.

"I'll be back soon, Mimi. I promise," said Mrs. Greenbaum. Then she gathered some clothes and folded them neatly into a large shopping bag. She placed her pillow and a bag with a half-finished knit scarf in another shopping bag. She put on her fluffy black fur coat and hat. "I'm ready," she said, bending over to pat Mimi on the head. "Be good, Mimi."

Mimi meowed and rubbed against her leg again.

"Let's go," said Mrs. Greenbaum.

"I'll carry your bags for you," said Ethan.

"Thank you. It's hard to carry bags and use my cane, too." She leaned over and blew out the candles, then headed for the door.

"Wait! I forgot something." Mrs. Greenbaum walked back to her kitchen and soon returned with a round, flowered tin. "Sugar cookies. They are especially good in a storm."

Ethan laughed. He led them out of the apartment, his flashlight lighting the way. It felt colder and darker in the building than it had before. The wind howled more fiercely, and the freezing rain pounded down harder as they headed up the stairs.

Mrs. Greenbaum held on to the railing as they slowly walked up to Ethan's apartment. At the landing she stopped, took a few deep breaths and then started walking again. It was clear that the climb up the steep stairs was hard for her, but she kept taking each step slowly, carefully leaning on her cane.

"Give me a minute to catch my breath," said Mrs. Greenbaum. She leaned against the wall outside Ethan's apartment and closed her eyes. Then she opened her eyes and said, "Now I'm ready."

Soon they were inside the apartment.

"Mrs. Greenbaum, it's good to see you," said Sylvie. "Come in and sit down,"

"I didn't want Mrs. Greenbaum to stay in her apartment alone," said Ethan.

Mrs. Greenbaum nodded. "It was hard to leave Mimi, but it's harder to be alone on such a terrible night with no electricity."

"I'm glad Ethan convinced you to come upstairs," said Sylvie.

"I invited Mrs. Greenbaum to sleep over," said Ethan. "I'm going to sleep on the couch and Mrs. Greenbaum can have my room."

"Of course. Great idea. Excuse me, I need to sit down."

"You look pale, Sylvie," said Mrs. Greenbaum, sitting down on the couch beside her. "How are you feeling?"

"I'm a little light-headed. It must be the weather. The damp and cold are getting to me, too. I guess I've been working too long on this ad."

"Have you eaten anything today?"

"Not much. Maybe I'll have some soup now.

I've come up with a way to warm it up. It's not perfect but it works."

Sylvie pointed to a large red fondue pot she and Jon had received as a wedding gift. She'd placed it on their dining-room table and lit the candle underneath to heat up a pot of homemade vegetable soup. "It should be warm enough to eat in a while."

"What a clever idea," said Mrs. Greenbaum.

"Hey, maybe we can have chocolate fondue for dessert," said Ethan. "We have apples, pears and chocolate."

"I'm not feeling hungry for chocolate tonight," said Sylvie, "but you could make some dessert for you and Mrs. Greenbaum after."

"Soup and fondue! What a combination," said Mrs. Greenbaum, laughing.

"I can make sandwiches to go with the soup, too. How's tuna?" Sylvie stood up, but then quickly sat down again.

"Why don't I make the sandwiches?" said Mrs. Greenbaum. "Ethan, come help me. You should take it easy, Sylvie. Stay warm with a blanket."

Sylvie nodded and leaned back against a large grey-and-red pillow on the couch. She pulled a blanket over her lap.

Ethan and Mrs. Greenbaum made tuna sandwiches in the kitchen. The narrow room was lit by a row of candles on a shelf near the refrigerator.

When the sandwiches were ready, Ethan brought them into the dining room on a platter. He sat down at the table with Mrs. Greenbaum as the candles flickered around them.

Sylvie walked over to join them.

"Such beautiful candles," said Mrs. Greenbaum.

"Thank you. I've always admired your silver candlesticks. Did you bring them from Russia?" asked Sylvie. Mrs. Greenbaum nodded. "They survived the war — like me," she said. "My mother hid them in her big fur coat when we escaped from the Nazis. We walked through dense forests and hid in a farmer's barn for almost a year. We were lucky to be helped by that kind farmer and his family. The candlesticks stayed with us the whole time."

"They're lovely."

"I polish them every week. I make them shine like a mirror — just like my mother did. And every time I light them, I remember my parents and the kindness of the farmer and his family."

Sylvie wiped tears from her eyes. "What a wonderful memory."

"Friends help us get through tough times, don't they?" said Mrs. Greenbaum. "I am happy to be with friends tonight."

"We're glad you're here, too," said Ethan, as they finished their soup and sandwiches. "Does anyone want chocolate fondue?"

"Chocolate fondue would be too much for me tonight," said Mrs. Greenbaum. "But what about some sugar cookies?" She opened her tin. "Ethan?"

"Yes, please." Ethan bit into one of the star-shaped cookies. "These are good."

"Sylvie? How about a cookie?" asked Mrs. Greenbaum.

"I'll have one. Your cookies are delicious."

"And one for me, too," said Mrs. Greenbaum. "Then I'm going to sit on the couch and knit." She pulled out the pink-and-red scarf she was working on.

"How will you see what you're doing?" asked Ethan, munching on a second cookie.

"I can knit even in the dark. My fingers know where to go even if I don't look."

"Mrs. Greenbaum, I hope you'll excuse me. I'm feeling tired. I think I'll go to bed now," said Sylvie.

"Of course. Feel better. I hope tomorrow is a brighter day for us all."

CHAPTER EIGHT

Ethan shivered and opened his eyes.

It was no use. He couldn't sleep.

He wore pyjamas, a heavy sweatshirt, two pairs of socks, gloves and a tuque, but he was still cold. He lay on the blanket he'd tucked around the cushions of the leather couch and wrapped himself tighter in the two thick blankets covering him. But the cold still reached him.

Mrs. Greenbaum's loud snoring and the pop and boom of ice crashing down had kept him up, too. It was the longest night he could remember.

He reached for the flashlight beside the couch and checked his watch.

Two a.m.!

He turned to his side and put a pillow over his

ears. He tried to tune out the noise, but it was no use.

Bang. Crash. Snort.

He'd tossed and turned on the couch since he'd gone to bed at ten. He kept pulling the blankets tighter around him, but it didn't help. No matter what he did, he couldn't get warm.

He flung off the blankets, then wrapped one around his shoulders and walked over to peer out the window. The glass was as frozen as an iceberg.

He stumbled back toward the couch, but a loud crack followed by a giant popping sound made him trip over a stool. He righted himself as something exploded against the window.

What was that? Ethan pictured the whole house coated in ice. What if the roof caved in? He'd once heard of a house where heavy ice and snow had caused the roof to collapse and everyone inside was hurt. Someone even died.

Boom! Crack!

It sounded like fireworks. He waited for more popping and crashing sounds, but it was quiet.

His teeth chattered as he sank back into the couch. He closed his eyes and tried to think of a picnic in the park on a beautiful sunny day. He tried to picture himself playing ball with his friends and swimming in a crystal-clear lake. He loved doing all those things, but tonight he couldn't imagine any of them. All he could think about was the wind banging against the window and the ice crashing down from the roof.

He was so tired. He yawned as he pulled the blankets higher on his shoulders. He yanked his tuque down over his cold ears.

✳   ✳   ✳

"Ethan. Ethan."

It was Sylvie. Her voice sounded far away. He must have finally fallen asleep.

Ethan opened his eyes. A sliver of light shone

through the still-frozen windows. His throat felt sore. He sneezed. Once. Twice. Three times.

"Ethan," said Sylvie. "It's eight. How did you sleep?"

"Not well. I was freezing." Ethan sneezed again. "I think I might be coming down with something."

"I didn't sleep much last night either. I kept shivering. Don't go to school today, even if it's open. You shouldn't be out in the freezing rain."

Ethan sat up. Why did Sylvie always talk to him like he was three years old? Yeah, he wasn't feeling great. His body ached and he felt as tired as if he'd been lugging around a box of bricks, but he didn't need Sylvie to baby him.

He was glad Mrs. Greenbaum was there so he didn't have to stay alone with Sylvie all day.

He fell back against his pillow. "I'm too tired to move. Even if there's school, I bet almost nobody will be there." He shivered and yanked his blankets up higher. "Is Mrs. Greenbaum up?"

"I heard her moving around in your room. She's probably getting dressed. I can warm up some milk in the fondue pot so we can have something hot to drink."

"I don't like warm milk," said Ethan, rubbing his eyes.

"How about warm milk with chocolate syrup?" said Sylvie.

Ethan nodded. "That's better. The milk is on the balcony, right?"

Sylvie nodded. "Can you get it while I look for the syrup?"

"Sure." Ethan sat up and tossed the blankets off. He walked over to the balcony and pulled the door handle. The door wouldn't move. He pulled harder. Nothing. He tried again and again until the door finally creaked open. He leaned over and tried to lift off the top of the cooler, but it was covered in a thick crust of ice.

"I can't open it. It's totally frozen," said Ethan.

"Here, use this," said Sylvie, handing him a screwdriver.

Ethan stuck it under the lid of the cooler, which wouldn't budge. The ice was as solid as a brick. He grabbed the screwdriver with both hands and started chipping away at the ice under the lid. "Got it!" Ethan pried open the lid and pulled out the milk. It too was frozen. He hurried inside with it.

Mrs. Greenbaum opened Ethan's bedroom door. She wore her hat and her winter coat over her clothes.

"How did you sleep?" asked Ethan.

"Not well, I'm afraid. Your bed is comfortable, but the cold was terrible, even with the blankets around me. I finally slept in my coat, hat and gloves, but I was still cold. How is out today?"

"It's still bad outside. I'll turn on the radio for more news."

"Much of the city has lost power, and power may go off at any time for those who currently have it," said

the announcer. *"The storm is not letting up. The city's pumping stations are affected by the storm and there may be a shortage of water. If you still have water, fill your bathtubs.*

"Shelters are being opened . . ."

Sylvie rolled her eyes and sighed. "No water? What next?" She leaned back against the big living-room chair and rubbed her belly.

CHAPTER NINE

"How are you feeling, Sylvie?" asked Mrs. Greenbaum.

"Okay. I'm a bit better. But I didn't get much sleep. Ethan, can you fill the bathtub with water for me? And some pitchers, too. There's some bottled water in the fridge, but we don't want to take chances."

"Okay," said Ethan.

He hurried to the bathroom and turned on the tap in the tub. He filled a pitcher and two large bowls with water and placed them on the kitchen counter.

"How about peanut-butter sandwiches with honey for breakfast?" said Sylvie.

"That sounds delicious," said Mrs. Greenbaum.

"This is my first time eating breakfast in gloves," said Ethan.

After breakfast Sylvie curled up in the big living-room chair and bundled herself in a blanket. "I'm going to call your dad," she told Ethan. She picked up the phone on the side table. "Oh no."

"What's the matter?' asked Ethan.

"The phone is dead. The wires must be down." Sylvie's lips quivered as she put down the phone. She sniffed back tears. "Sorry. It's just . . ."

Mrs. Greenbaum put her arm around Sylvie's shoulders. "I understand. I was hoping today would be better. But the weather will get better soon, I'm sure of it. The storm can't last forever."

Sylvie drew the blanket closer around her. "I'm so tired. I think I may nap for a while. It wasn't a good night."

"Not for any of us," said Mrs. Greenbaum. "I'm going down to my apartment to check on Mimi. If I'm away for too long she gets into mischief."

"Don't forget to fill your bathtub with water," Ethan reminded her.

"I won't."

"Please come back later. We'll put something together for lunch and supper," said Sylvie.

Mrs. Greenbaum nodded. "Of course I'll be back. I don't want you two to be alone either, especially if you're not feeling well, Sylvie. Maybe the power will be back on by then. I'm glad you have a radio."

"I'll walk you downstairs," said Ethan. "I can hold the flashlight."

"Thank you."

"Don't stay away long, Ethan. You have a cold and you didn't sleep well. Maybe you should take a nap, too," said Sylvie.

"I feel much better now. It's just a cold. I don't need a nap," said Ethan, gritting his teeth. He grabbed his flashlight and followed Mrs. Greenbaum out the door.

"You sound angry with Sylvie," said Mrs. Greenbaum, as he led the way down the stairs.

"She always treats me like a little kid. She's always telling me what to do. She's not my mother."

"She cares about you. She's never been a mother before and she's tired. Give her time."

"I don't want to talk about it, okay?"

"Okay. I know that you'll figure it out. Here we are." Mrs. Greenbaum unlocked her door. "I'll be upstairs in a little while."

"Promise?"

"I promise. Maybe we'll play a game of checkers."

"I haven't played in a long time but, sure, we can play."

Ethan waved to Mrs. Greenbaum and headed back upstairs.

When he got back to the apartment he found Sylvie asleep in the chair.

He sat down on the couch, draped a blanket

around his shoulders and picked up a magazine from the coffee table. He began reading an article about the Montreal Expos, but it was hard to keep his mind on the words. Ethan closed his eyes and imagined himself in Olympic Stadium on a warm spring day, eating a hot dog slathered with mustard and a big basket of sizzling french fries. *A hot dog and french fries would taste so good.*

So good . . .

* * *

"Ethan. Ethan, wake up. We should check on Mrs. Greenbaum."

Ethan's eyes popped open. He'd fallen asleep! He shivered as he pulled himself up on the couch. He was wearing his winter jacket, a tuque and gloves, but he was still freezing. It was so cold his hands had gone numb and his toes felt frozen even inside his double socks.

He looked at his watch. It was one o'clock. He'd slept for over three hours!

"Were you asleep all this time, too?" he asked Sylvie.

"I slept till noon. You looked so exhausted, I didn't want to wake you. But I'm worried about Mrs. Greenbaum. I thought she'd be back here by now. Can you go down and see if she's all right?"

Sylvie suddenly grabbed the side of the chair.

"What's the matter?" asked Ethan.

"Just a little light-headed again. It will pass once I have something to eat. It's probably nothing."

"I'll be back soon," said Ethan, before sliding on his winter boots, grabbing his flashlight and heading out the door.

CHAPTER TEN

Ethan knocked on Mrs. Greenbaum's door.

No one answered. He knocked again and again.

Nothing.

"Mrs. Greenbaum, please answer the door!" he called out, but no one responded.

His heart began to pound. *Why isn't she answering?*

"Mrs. Greenbaum, please come to the door!" Ethan called, as he banged harder and harder.

Meow. Meow. Meow.

It was Mimi. He'd never heard the cat meow so long or so loudly.

Where's Mrs. Greenbaum?

Ethan rattled the doorknob. As he did, the door

sprung open! Mrs. Greenbaum usually locked her door, but she hadn't this time. Her outdoor cane was in the umbrella stand by the front door. She never went anywhere without it! She had to be somewhere inside! But where? He dashed into the dark apartment.

He aimed his flashlight up and down the hall. Mrs. Greenbaum wasn't there. He called her name over and over. No answer.

What's that smell? He sniffed. *Smoke! Where's it coming from?*

Ethan shone his light ahead and sniffed again. "Mrs. Greenbaum!"

There was no smoke in the hall or the living room. It was coming from . . . Mrs. Greenbaum's bedroom!

He raced over to the door and pushed it open. The air inside the bedroom was heavy with smoke. He gagged and coughed. It was hard to breathe.

"Mrs. Greenbaum! Are you there? Are you okay?" he sputtered, coughing.

There was no answer. What was burning? Where was Mrs. Greenbaum? His heart pounded so hard he could barely think. He flashed his light up and down the room, across the walls, up to the ceiling.

The smoke was getting thicker and stronger. He couldn't stay in the room much longer. He couldn't breathe.

He had to find Mrs. Greenbaum.

"Mrs. Greenbaum!" He scanned the room again with his light.

Flames suddenly leapt from the open closet, eating through clothes and bags and boxes.

"Fire!" yelled Ethan.

A muffled sound came from across the room. "Mrs. Greenbaum, where are you?" He whipped around and pointed his light toward the sound.

Mrs. Greenbaum lay on the floor beside her

bed. Her leg was twisted and she was moaning and coughing.

Ethan didn't know what to do. The fire was starting to spread beyond the closet and smoke was filling the room. He had to get himself and Mrs. Greenbaum out of there.

Ethan coughed as he hurried over to Mrs.

Greenbaum. He leaned over her. Her eyes were closed but she was breathing.

"Mrs. Greenbaum, are you okay?" he asked, taking her hand. "Can you move? Talk to me."

She opened her eyes and coughed.

"Ethan." Mrs. Greenbaum's voice was weak and raspy.

"Can you sit up? Can you move? "Ethan asked, choking on smoke.

"My leg. Can't . . . breathe." Mrs. Greenbaum closed her eyes. She coughed and gagged.

Ethan had to get her out of the house, but how? He couldn't lift her up. Her leg was twisted and she couldn't move. She needed air and so did he. He was starting to feel dizzy.

Meow!

Mimi dashed out from under Mrs. Greenbaum's writing table, pushing aside an old-fashioned wooden chair. The cat scurried out of the room as the chair rolled toward Ethan and Mrs. Greenbaum.

The chair. Yes! That's it!

If Ethan could get Mrs. Greenbaum onto the chair, he could push her out of the smoke-filled room.

"Mrs. Greenbaum, I'm going to help you into the chair and then move you out. Okay?"

Mrs. Greenbaum opened her eyes and coughed. She coughed so hard she shook and tears rolled down her cheeks. She nodded yes and coughed again. She pointed to her throat.

She was having more trouble breathing!

"Okay. I'm going to put my arms under your arms. Try and help me so I can lift you into the chair."

Mrs. Greenbaum nodded and put her hands on the floor, ready to push herself up.

"One, two, three, up!" said Ethan.

Mrs. Greenbaum groaned. Ethan tried with every ounce of his strength, but he couldn't lift her high enough to reach the chair.

He coughed. His eyes stung from the smoke. His head was spinning and a wave of nausea rose up in his throat. He was afraid he'd pass out if he didn't get out soon.

What do I do?

The fire was spreading, consuming everything in its path.

CHAPTER ELEVEN

"Mrs. Greenbaum, we have to try again," croaked Ethan. He coughed so hard his chest hurt. It was hard to talk or breathe. He felt sick to his stomach. There was so much smoke he could barely see anything ahead of him.

Mrs. Greenbaum nodded and pushed her hands into the floor as Ethan lifted her again. They both fell back, coughing and gasping for air.

"We . . . can't give up. We have to get outside," said Ethan. "One, two, three, up!" Ethan pulled Mrs. Greenbaum as hard and as high as he could.

This time she fell into the chair.

"Let's go!" Ethan thrust the chair forward and out of the room. He shoved it toward the living room as flames engulfed the bedroom.

The living room was filling up with smoke, too. He pushed the chair down the hall and out of the apartment. He had to get them outside. But how could he lift a heavy chair and Mrs. Greenbaum down the three icy steps to the street?

He had to try. It was their only chance. The flames were moving quickly. Soon the whole house might be engulfed and then . . .

Oh no! Sylvie! He'd almost forgotten. She was still upstairs.

"Fire!" he shouted up the stairs. "Sylvie! Fire! Get out!"

"Ethan!" Sylvie yelled down from the second-floor landing. Her voice was hoarse. "I'm coming down. Are you okay? Is Mrs. Greenbaum okay?"

"Hurry downstairs!" Ethan yelled back. "We have to get outside fast."

Sylvie staggered down the stairs, clinging to the railing and coughing.

"We have to move quickly," Ethan said when Sylvie reached the first floor. "Mrs. Greenbaum can't walk. I can't lift her and the chair down the front steps. It's too heavy."

"I'll help you. We'll do it together." Sylvie grabbed Ethan's hand and gave it a quick squeeze. "Come on. Let's go."

Ethan nodded and squeezed Sylvie's hand back. How could he have forgotten that she was in the house, too? "Thanks, Sylvie," said Ethan.

"Mrs. Greenbaum," said Sylvie, "Ethan and I are going to get you out of here. Are you okay?"

"Not so good," muttered Mrs. Greenbaum, closing her eyes and wincing. She coughed and gagged. "Can't breathe. Pain."

Ethan ran ahead and opened the front door. As soon as he did, Mimi streaked across the floor and dashed out into the cold.

There was no time to look for her. Ethan pushed the chair toward the door. A blast of freezing air blew into the smoke-filled house. He guided the chair to the top of the first step. Sylvie quickly followed.

Ethan placed his hands under one side of the chair, and Sylvie placed her hands under the other side.

"Here we go, Mrs. Greenbaum. Hold on tight. One, two, three, up," said Ethan.

Ethan strained every muscle in his arms, legs and shoulders to lift the heavy chair and Mrs. Greenbaum. Sylvie's jaw tightened with the effort. The chair tilted back and swayed. It looked like Mrs. Greenbaum would tumble onto the hard, ice-covered ground. Quickly they straightened the chair.

"Stop. Rest here," Sylvie moaned, as they set the chair down on the wide second step. "I'm out of breath."

"Sure," said Ethan. He was having trouble breathing, too. His chest hurt and he couldn't stop coughing. The wind blew icy pellets into his eyes. He shivered as he and Sylvie held the chair in place on the second step.

"This is hard," said Sylvie.

"I know." Every part of Ethan ached. He glanced back at the house. Flames lit up Mrs. Greenbaum's living room. He could see them even through the frozen window. He could smell smoke even in the frigid air.

"Thank you," murmured Mrs. Greenbaum, opening her eyes and looking up at Ethan and Sylvie. "Mimi?"

"She's outside but I don't know where," said Ethan. "Don't worry. She'll be fine. She's a smart cat. Sylvie, one more step and then down to the sidewalk."

"Okay. I'm ready," said Sylvie, placing her hands under the chair again.

"One, two, three. Go!" said Ethan.

With all their might, they lifted Mrs. Greenbaum to the last step and then quickly down to the frozen sidewalk.

But when they placed the chair on the sidewalk, their hands slipped off and it rolled across the ice. Ethan raced forward. He grabbed the arms of the chair, stopping it from moving.

"Phew. That was close!" said Ethan, gripping the chair to steady it. His heart was racing. "Are you okay, Mrs. Greenbaum?"

Mrs. Greenbaum only groaned.

"Ethan!" cried Sylvie.

Ethan glanced at his stepmother. Her face was contorted in pain.

"Ethan," she groaned. "I . . . I . . ."

"What's the matter?" asked Ethan, touching her arm.

"Bad pain. The baby. I need help. Now."

CHAPTER TWELVE

What do I do?

Something was wrong with Sylvie and the baby. Mrs. Greenbaum was hurt and her breathing was getting worse. Ethan glanced up and down the street. No one was outside. Nothing was moving. They were alone on the street.

He had to find help somewhere else. But how could he leave Sylvie and Mrs. Greenbaum in the freezing cold with a fire raging behind them? What if the fire spread quickly and . . .

"The baby," Sylvie moaned.

He had no choice. He had to find someone *now*. But who could help them?

Rafi's mom! She was a nurse. His mom could

stay with Sylvie and Mrs. Greenbaum while Ethan went for more help on the main street.

"I'm going to get Rafi's mom to help you, Sylvie. I'll be right back."

"Please hurry." Sylvie bit her lip and clung to the back of Mrs. Greenbaum's chair.

Ethan hurried ahead as a wave of dizziness rolled over him. He stopped to take a breath. Pellets of freezing rain flew into his face and eyes. The ice stung like needles against his cheek. It was hard to breathe as it hammered him in the face. It was hard to walk on the slippery frozen ground.

The houses on their block were draped in thick white ice. They looked like they were splattered in layers of icing. Icicles the size of swords hung down from the roofs, the entrances, the balconies and the window ledges.

Trees were bent over. Some had snapped in half. Huge limbs had crashed down on top of frozen cars, garbage cans and mailboxes. The cars that weren't damaged lay abandoned and useless under the heavy ice.

Cables and wires were stuck to the ground. A shopping cart stood on the street like a statue encased in ice.

The streets looked like a world of endless winter — a world where all the people had disappeared.

Ethan shivered. The cold pierced through his jacket and pants. He peered around, but it was hard to see anything ahead of him or behind him. He pulled the hood of his jacket tighter to stop the icy pellets from blinding him further.

The ground was as slick as glass. Every step made him feel like he'd slide across the ice on his back. Ethan's boots had good traction, but he still couldn't stop himself from slipping.

He stepped over broken tree limbs and branches. He crawled over ice mounds. He jumped out of the way when chunks of ice crashed down from above.

He could barely feel his fingers. They were numb despite his thick gloves. His face stung from the biting cold, even though he'd pulled his tuque down lower on his face.

The wind whistled in his ears, and the freezing rain kept coming down as he crossed the street to Rafi's building. He circled frozen cars until he found a narrow patch of level ground to walk on. It was slow and hard, but finally he stood in front of the building.

He was about to press the buzzer when it hit him: he couldn't ring the bell and speak to Rafi on the intercom! The bell wouldn't work without power.

He leaned against the ice-covered brick building. *Why didn't I think of this before? What do I do now?*

He banged hard on the door, hoping that someone inside would somehow hear him. But no one answered. He drew closer to the door, hoping to hear footsteps, but the only sound he heard was the pinging of ice pellets.

He had to look for help on the main street instead! It was two blocks away.

If only he weren't so tired, so achy. Every part of him was as sore as if he'd run for kilometres.

Ethan forced himself to move. He climbed back

over the ice mounds in front of Rafi's building. He was about to cross the street when a chunk of ice crashed down in front of him.

Ethan stumbled and fell to the ground.

CHAPTER THIRTEEN

Ethan's back, leg and arms hit jagged ice. His ankle twisted in the fall. The pain was sharp and throbbing. He couldn't move. He couldn't think. His head ached. Ice pellets hit him in the face as he lay on the uneven frozen ground.

Every breath hurt his chest. Every swallow hurt his throat. He tried to push himself up with his arms, but the pain in his ankle was so intense he could barely move.

He slid back down to the ground. He moved his right leg and then slowly his left. His ankle hurt each time he moved it.

Get up. Sylvie and Mrs. Greenbaum need you.

He sucked in his breath, pulled his hood closer to

his face and tried again to move. This time a sharp pain in his side stopped him.

He sank down on the ice again.

What now?

He peered around. There was no one in sight. The city felt like a ghost town.

Ethan closed his eyes. Every movement hurt, but he couldn't stay there on the frozen ground. He couldn't stop shivering as the ice pellets fell like hail, hitting his face, his back — everywhere.

Then he thought about Sylvie and Mrs. Greenbaum waiting for help to come. He pushed himself up with all his might. He bit his lip and took a step forward. Pain shot through him. He stopped and took another breath, followed by another step.

Go. Go. Breathe. Take more steps.

"One, two . . . Ow . . ." He winced.

Don't stop. Keep going.

"Three, four," he counted his steps out loud. "Five, six."

Keep counting. Keep going.

"Seven, eight."

It seemed to take forever to walk just one block.

His teeth began to chatter as he made his way slowly and painfully down the street. All he heard was his teeth and the ice crashing down around him.

"Nine, ten, eleven," he chanted.

Each step took all his concentration. Each step felt like a knife was being pushed deeper into his chest.

His body wanted to stop and rest, but he knew if he stopped now he might never have the energy to get up. He finally reached the main road and looked up and down it. There were no cars on the road; there were no people on the street. He leaned against a frozen car, closed his eyes and tried to think. What could he do? Where could he go?

And then he heard a voice. "Hey, kid? Are you all right?"

Ethan opened his eyes. It was a policeman in a patrol car! Another policeman sat beside him.

"I need help!" said Ethan. "There was a fire. My neighbour's hurt. My stepmother's having a baby!"

"Slow down. Get in the car and tell us what's happened and where you live. I'm Sergeant Grant. This is Officer Leon."

Ethan hobbled over to the police car and opened the door. He slid into the back seat. A blast of warm air enveloped him.

"Are you okay? Are you hurt?"

Ethan coughed. "I fell on the ice. My ankle hurts. Please hurry."

As he snapped on his seat belt, Ethan quickly told the policemen about the fire, Mrs. Greenbaum and Sylvie, and where he'd left them.

"I'll radio for fire and ambulance help. Meanwhile, let's go to your place and see what we can do."

The police car bumped down the icy, rutted street. Exhausted, Ethan put his head back against the car seat. He hoped he hadn't taken too long to find help.

"The reception isn't good," said Sergeant Grant, after trying three times to relay his message. "I hear a lot of crackling sounds and a faint voice at the other end. Fingers crossed that they heard me."

Just then the police car veered sharply left onto a side street.

"Sorry about the bumpy drive, but there's not much we can do." said Sergeant Grant.

Suddenly the car was spinning on the ice. Ethan fell forward. The car spun again and again. It was like an out-of-control merry-go-round. Then with a thud, the car hit an ice hill.

CHAPTER FOURTEEN

Officer Leon leaned back in his seat and clutched the steering wheel. "That was a wild ride. Sorry about that," he said. "Hold on to the seat, everybody. It might not be easy to pull the car off this iceberg."

Officer Leon revved the engine. The tires spun as he tried to back away, but the car wouldn't move off the ice. He tried again and again. Nothing happened.

"Get ready. I'm going to rock the car back and forth."

Ethan held on to the seat as the officer reversed. The car jerked forward, then backwards.

When would they get off this ice hill? It had to have been over a half-hour since he'd left Sylvie and Mrs. Greenbaum. And what if the message for help didn't go through or the ambulance couldn't get down their street? It was a mess of ice, frozen cars and broken trees.

"Here we go one more time!" Officer Leon gripped the wheel and rocked the car back and forth until it finally inched forward.

"Let's go!" he said. He slammed on the gas.

The tires screeched, but the car slid off the hill and bumped down the street.

The police car rumbled over the ice. It veered right, swerved and spun left and bumped down a different side street. It hit another ice hill, and Ethan held his breath as Officer Leon drove it back and forth again. This time it slid off the ice with more ease.

They were only a block from his house.

Ethan's heart pounded so hard he could barely breathe as the car zigzagged around fallen branches and wires stuck to the ground before turning onto his block. They were halfway down when the clang of fire-truck sirens pierced the air. Ethan looked out the back window. The fire truck was right behind them.

Ethan could see his house clearly now! The fire was still raging. It was bigger than before, but there was no one on the sidewalk out front.

Where were Mrs. Greenbaum and Sylvie? Did the ambulance come?

The police car skidded to a stop. The fire truck stopped behind them and the firefighters jumped out. They raced over to check out the house.

"Wait in the car, Ethan," said Sergeant Grant. "It's dangerous to get any closer. We'll find out what's happened."

Sergeant Grant and Officer Leon got out of the car. They quickly spoke to the firefighters.

Ethan's stomach knotted as he waited for them to return. In a few minutes Sergeant Grant was back. "The first floor looks bad, but they hope they can stop the fire from spreading to other houses. They don't know the condition of the rest of the house yet. Meanwhile, we're taking you to the nearest hospital. The firefighters don't know anything about your stepmom and neighbour. They've had problems with their radios and phones today, too."

The policemen got back in the car and revved the motor. The car bumped back over the icy, deserted streets. It took a roundabout route to avoid streets blocked by ice, cars, fallen trees and wires. The trip to the hospital felt like it was taking forever.

"There's the hospital." Officer Leon finally announced.

The wide building was draped in thick white ice. A big sign in front flashed, but the light looked dim — like it would go off at any moment.

The tires squealed as the car came to a stop in front of the hospital. The policemen opened their doors and hurried out. They opened Ethan's door. He took a step forward and cried out.

"That ankle is bad, isn't it?" asked Officer Leon.

"Yeah," said Ethan, gritting his teeth.

"Why don't we get you a wheelchair?"

"No. Please. I can manage," said Ethan.

Sergeant Grant and Officer Leon looked at each other and nodded.

"Okay. Lean on me and I'll help you hop your way in," said Officer Leon.

"I'll go inside and see what I can find out about your stepmother and your neighbour," said Sergeant Grant. "If they're not at this hospital, we'll see if we can find out where they are."

CHAPTER FIFTEEN

Sergeant Grant went inside as Officer Leon put his arm around Ethan's shoulders. Ethan placed his arm around the officer's waist.

"Here we go!" said Officer Leon, taking a step. Ethan hopped beside him. It was hard and tiring to maintain balance on the icy walkway to the hospital, but Officer Leon's arm kept him steady.

Finally they were inside. Officer Leon helped Ethan to a bench. "I'm getting you a wheelchair," he said.

Ethan yanked off his soggy tuque and dripping gloves. He unzipped his jacket and looked around.

Families were camped out on benches. A little boy cried and clung to his mother. Two little girls raced across the hall and almost collided with

Officer Leon, who was pushing a wheelchair toward Ethan.

"Come on. Let's get you signed in. They're busy, so it may be a wait."

Officer Leon helped Ethan into the wheelchair. Then he wheeled him down the hall to the emergency room. It was teeming with people waiting to be seen. After giving the receptionist their information, they were directed to wait.

"As soon as Sergeant Grant is back, we're going to have to get back on the road," said Officer Leon. "I've spoken to the nurse, and she promised she would look out for you until you find your stepmother and your neighbour. Right after my shift, I'll come back and check on you. You're on my way home."

"Thanks for everything," said Ethan.

"Ethan?"

Ethan couldn't believe it! "Rafi! What are you doing here?" he said.

"Jose's cold got worse. He had a really high fever. We came here about two hours ago. Jose is with a doctor now. What happened to you?"

Ethan explained, then introduced Rafi to Officer Leon.

"I'm glad Ethan won't be alone when we have to take off," said Officer Leon. "Here's Sergeant Grant."

Sergeant Grant hurried over. "I have news," he told Ethan. "The ambulance brought your stepmother and Mrs. Greenbaum here about a half-hour ago. They said they made it just in time. Your stepmother is having her baby now. Getting help for them as quickly as you did made all the difference."

"Are Sylvie and Mrs. Greenbaum . . . okay?" asked Ethan. "And the baby?"

"The nurse promised to let you know as soon as she has more news."

"Where is Mrs. Greenbaum? Can I see her?"

"She's still here in emergency, waiting for a bed. I'll ask if an attendant can take you."

Sergeant Grant spoke to the nurse, and soon Ethan was wheeled over to a small cubicle.

"Ethan!" Mrs. Greenbaum was lying on a gurney with her leg in a splint. Her voice was still raspy. "I am so happy to see you. If it wasn't for you . . ."

Ethan wheeled himself over and held her hand.

"Are you in pain?" he asked.

"They gave me medicine. It helps. You know about Sylvie and the baby?"

"Yes. I'm waiting for news. I have to let Dad know."

"This is all my fault. If only I had changed my fire alarm batteries. If only I hadn't gone looking for an extra flashlight in the closet, then the fire wouldn't have started."

"What happened?"

"The battery in my flashlight died, so I took a

candle to look for another flashlight. It was dark and I didn't see Mimi. I tripped over her and dropped the candle. Thank goodness you came when you did."

"Is your leg broken?"

"Yes. They will operate on it soon, but they say I will be able to walk again after rehabilitation."

"You'll get back on your feet. Nothing stops you, Mrs. Greenbaum."

Mrs. Greenbaum stroked Ethan's hair. "Why are you in a wheelchair?"

"I messed up my ankle on the ice and I might have cracked a rib. They're going to check it out."

"Oy. So we will practise walking on crutches together."

Ethan smiled. "We can help each other. I'd better call my dad now and tell him what's happened. I wish he were here."

CHAPTER SIXTEEN

January 9, 1998

Ethan's dad was finally able to travel. He'd be here at any moment! Ethan scanned the front door of the hospital.

There he was!

Ethan's dad raced over to the front reception desk where Ethan was waiting. "Ethan!" he called, hugging him.

"Dad! I'm so glad you're here."

"I wish I could have been here days ago. How's your ankle?"

"Much better. I'm lucky that it was just sprained."

"And you've been okay staying with Rafi's family?"

"Yeah, his aunt has a generator at her place, so it's been warm."

"Let's go upstairs and see Sylvie. I want to meet your sister!"

A few minutes later they were on the maternity floor.

Sylvie was sitting in bed, propped up against pillows, when they walked in.

"Jon!" she exclaimed.

Ethan's dad rushed over to hug her. Ethan followed. Sylvie stretched her hand out to him. He took it and smiled.

"Ethan has been so great through all this," she said. "If it wasn't for him . . ." Sylvie's eyes filled with tears.

"I know. I'm proud of him. And the baby? How's she doing today?" asked Ethan's dad.

"She's doing well. Better every day. She was tiny but she's a fighter. They're still monitoring her in the Neonatal Intensive Care Unit. I hope we can take her home soon," said Sylvie.

"I found a furnished house to rent for the time being. Most of our furniture is gone," said Ethan's dad.

"And Mrs. Greenbaum lost everything," said Ethan.

"No. I didn't lose everything."

Everyone looked up. A nurse was wheeling Mrs. Greenbaum into the room.

"We are all here together, and that is what counts. I am so grateful for your friendship and help," said Mrs. Greenbaum.

Ethan's dad gave Mrs. Greenbaum a hug. "As soon as you are out of rehab, you can stay with us. Our new house is large. We can help you find a new apartment when you're better."

Mrs. Greenbaum choked back tears. "Thank you."

"You're part of our family," said Ethan.

"That means . . . everything. And when I'm better, I hope I can help with the baby."

Sylvie smiled. "That would be wonderful."

"Could you also bake us a big batch of sugar cookies when you're better?" asked Ethan.

"Of course!" said Mrs. Greenbaum, squeezing Ethan's hand. "I will bake you the *best* sugar cookies you have ever tasted!"

Author's Note

In December 2013 much of Ontario — including Toronto, where I live — was hit by a terrible ice storm. It was a cold, miserable experience, and it gave me a sense of how nasty an ice storm can be. Yet the storm I lived through didn't have the intensity and long-term damage of the one that pummelled Montreal in 1998. The devastating effects of that ice storm surprised even the residents of Montreal, Quebec, who are used to tough winters.

The storm began on January 4, 1998, and continued for over three days. Freezing rain and ice pellets hit much of eastern Ontario, huge areas of southern Quebec, northern New York and northern New England.

The storm caused massive power outages,

damaged water plants, broke trees and forced transportation, schools and businesses in most of Montreal to close for over a week. Falling ice was a major problem, injuring people and damaging cars and buildings. Residents were urged to boil water before using it because filtration plants were crippled. Bridges and tunnels into Montreal were also closed, further isolating the city.

The south shore of Montreal was hit so hard it was called "the triangle of darkness." More than 500,000 people in the area were without power for days and had to scramble for shelter. Some people lost power for up to a month.

Many people were forced into crowded shelters. Others, including many of the elderly, suffered alone through days of brutal cold and darkness.

A steep drop in temperature and strong, gusting winds made the problems even worse. Not only were buildings, streets and trees damaged, but many people were injured and even killed.

Some people died of carbon monoxide poisoning from using generators. Others developed hypothermia — a condition where body heat is lost rapidly due to extreme cold.

During the storm Montreal's main hospitals lost their primary power and had to rely on emergency generators to function. It was difficult for those who needed help to reach hospitals because of ice-blocked streets and fallen trees and debris. Many hospitals not only had to deal with injuries but also house people who had no power and no other place to go. In some cases hospital staff and their families were forced to camp out in the hospital for days.

Outside of Montreal barns collapsed, killing farm animals. Many maple trees were destroyed by the wind and ice, devastating the maple syrup industry. Orchards lost trees, and greenhouses were damaged, causing major financial losses.

Hydro workers, police, Red Cross volunteers, firefighters and the Canadian Forces helped repair power lines and rescue people caught in the storm. Some hydro repair technicians worked for sixteen hours at a time trying to restore power. There was so much to fix that crews from New England were called in to help.

The ice storm of 1998 was historic in the damage it inflicted on families and communities. While this story is a work of fiction, it represents some of the hardships people faced during the storm.

Downed trees made navigating Montreal's streets difficult and even dangerous.

About the Great Ice Storm of 1998

- Ice storms occur when warm air is caught between two layers of cold air. Snow that forms high in the atmosphere turns to rain as it falls through the layer of warm air. Then as the rain droplets enter the cool air layer below, they begin to cool very quickly and freeze when they hit a surface.

- Power outages hit some areas as early as January 5, as heavy ice accumulated on trees, poles and power lines.

- By January 6, about 650,000 Ontario and Quebec residents had lost power.

- By January 8, The Canadian Forces started arriving to help rescue people caught in the storm and provide basic services.

- On January 9, the crisis worsened, and much of Montreal lost its water supply when pumping stations failed in the storm.

- It wasn't until January 14, ten days after the storm began, that much of Montreal had its power restored.

- On January 22, more than 400,000 Quebecers were still without power.

- Twenty days after the ice storm began, three roofs in Montreal collapsed under the weight of the ice and the new snow that had fallen on top of it.

- On January 26, at least 60,000 Quebec households were still without power.

- On February 6, power was fully restored in Quebec.

- The estimated cost of the ice storm was over $5.4 billion.
- Thousands of people were homeless for weeks because of the ice storm. Hundreds were injured and approximately thirty people in Quebec died.

ALSO AVAILABLE

ISBN 978-1-4431-4638-8

In a matter of seconds, Alex's world is turned upside down. What started out as the perfect day to build an epic snow fort turns into his worst nightmare. Injured and disoriented, can Alex find his classmates trapped in the deadly snow?

ALSO AVAILABLE

SURVIVAL

Shipwreck!

FRIEDA WISHINSKY

SCHOLASTIC

ISBN 978-1-4431-4641-8

Albert and Grace feel a jolt. The *Empress of Ireland* begins to tilt. People scream. Stewards order passengers to head for the lifeboats. Water rushes into the ship as passengers race to the top deck. The ship tilts toward the water. Lifeboats crash down. Grace and Albert have no choice. They leap into the St. Lawrence River.

ALSO AVAILABLE

ISBN 978-1-4431-4644-9

Hurricane Hazel has been devastating the Caribbean and southern United States, but no one expects Hazel to reach Toronto. No one is prepared. When the Humber River overflows its banks, Michael's house is in danger of being swept away. Fleeing his home through the roof, Michael plummets into the freezing water. How will he make it out alive?